The Amulet Of Amser
The Case Of The Mona Lisa

by Yvonne Jones

ISBN-10: 0997025409
ISBN-13: 978-0-9970254-0-8

Text & illustrations copyright © 2015 by Yvonne Jones.

All rights reserved. Published by LHC Publishing.

Printed in the U.S.A.

DEDICATION

To all the little art lovers out there.

CONTENTS

ACKNOWLEDGMENTS

To my oldest little one, without whose tireless enthusiasm and support the writing of this book would have taken only half as long.

1
Visiting Gramps

Wen was so excited he was bouncing in his seat. He hadn't seen his grandfather in months. But now his school year was finally over and Wen was on his way to spend the entire summer with him. Gramps always had the most interesting stories, but this time was extra special. Gramps told Wen on the phone that he had a surprise for him. Wen had no idea what this surprise was all about, so he was bursting with excitement and couldn't wait to finally reach Gramps' house. The drive seemed to take forever. The roads wound through the dark forest, on and on, and the sky got darker and darker as the day wore on and the sun began to disappear behind the trees.

Gramps was a very interesting guy and Wen was always fascinated by his tales. He knew that Gramps had been all over the world. He always seemed a bit mysterious to Wen; full of secrets and past adventures.

"Are you sure you can handle an entire summer at Gramps'?" Dad asked him from the driver's seat. He was looking into the rearview mirror to get a glimpse of Wen. "You've never stayed away from Mom and me that long."

"No problem, Dad," Wen assured him, "Gramps and I will have a great time. Besides, Gramps said that he has a surprise for me. That will keep me busy the entire time."

Wen's dad smiled. Wen wondered if his dad knew

what the big surprise was, but he didn't get a chance to ask. They were here! Their car crunched up the steep, gravel-covered driveway to Gramps' curious-looking house. As they pulled up, Wen saw a shadow disappearing behind the bushes. *Probably just the neighbor's cat*, Wen thought.

2
All About Names

Woof! Woof! The next morning Wen was awakened by happy yapping and a very wet lick. "Minty! Stop that!" Wen giggled while trying to cover his face with his hands. Minty was Gramps' very energetic, chocolate-brown Terrier. She loved Wen. Nobody knew her real age, but she'd been with the family forever; for generations, it seemed. Wen picked her up and gently nudged her snout with his nose. Then he put her back on the floor.

"Alright, I'm up," Wen said while pulling his shirt over his head. He had been so tired and exhausted from the long drive the night before that he didn't even remember how he got to bed.

With Minty close behind, Wen hopped down the stairs. He smelled pancakes and bacon. "There you are," Gramps greeted him, a spatula in his hand and an apron wrapped around his waist. "Guess Minty did her job waking you up." Smiling, he loaded up a plate with pancakes and bacon and handed it to Wen. Wen sat at the kitchen table and drizzled syrup all over his plate before digging in.

Gramps took a couple of bites of his pancakes. Then he looked straight into Wen's eyes. After a few seconds of silence, he asked, "Did you ever wonder about your name, Wen? Or about your dad's? Or mine?"

Wen was puzzled. "My name?" he asked. He

poked his pancakes with his fork and thought about Gramps' odd question. "I guess Wendall is not very common. I mean, I don't know anybody else with my name. But I never really thought about it. Why?"

"Well," Wen's grandfather said, "your name, all our names, really – your dad's, mine, yours – were actually carefully chosen. All our ancestors' names are English and mean *Traveler*."

"Traveler?" Wen asked, crunching on his bacon. "So, Dad's name *Dwade* and your name *Faerwald*, mean Traveler?"

Wen's grandfather nodded. "Yes, and so does *Wendall*."

Wen looked surprised. Thinking about it, those names did seem a bit unusual compared to other people he knew. He stuffed the last piece of pancake into his mouth and chewed thoughtfully. "Why do all our names mean the same thing? Why are we named that way, Gramps?"

With a smile on his face, Gramps put the empty plates into the sink and motioned for Wen to follow him.

3
The Library

Gramps' house was a mysterious one, filled with odd nooks and hidden crannies. Wen's favorite room in the entire house was Gramps' library. It wasn't as big as Wen's school library, of course, but he always loved the smell of the old, leather-bound books that covered all four walls up to the very ceiling. He'd spent many hours in this room, sitting on Gramps' lap while his grandfather was reading one of the wondrous volumes to him.

"Take a seat," his grandfather said, after they entered the room. "I want to show you something."

The surprise! Wen quickly sat down, fidgeting with excitement as he watched Gramps. Carefully climbing the ladder propped against one of the shelves, Gramps grabbed a heavy-looking book from the very top. "I got this book from my grandfather when I was about your age," he said. "Your dad and I both agree that it's time for you to know."

What was Gramps talking about? "Know what?" Wen asked.

"Take a look," Gramps said, handing him the thick book.

Flipping through the pages, Wen didn't understand why his grandfather had given him this book. "It's just a bunch of stories about famous pieces of art,

Gramps. Just like all the other ones you've been reading to me ever since I was little. How is this one different?"

"It isn't," his grandfather answered. "All the books in this library are special. Very special."

Lowering himself onto the sofa beside his grandson, Gramps began to explain. "All the stories in this book, and in all the other books within this library, have been changed by members of the Amser family..." Gramps shifted in his seat. "All the pieces of art described in these books would be lost to all of us today if we hadn't traveled back in time to save them."

Wen looked confused. "What do you mean? How did you change these stories? And how did you save these pieces of art? I mean, what do you mean by *traveling in time to save them*?"

"What I mean, Wen," taking hold of Wen's hand, as though to make sure he'd understand what he was trying to tell him, Gramps answered, "is that some members of the Amser family can travel through time."

4
Is This A Dream?

"Let's not waste any time and I will show you." Gramps took another book off of the shelf beside him and passed it to Wen. Wen sat silently, stunned.

"Open it. I'll be right back," his grandfather said, jumping up and leaving the room.

Wen opened the book. "Gramps," he said, flipping through the pages. "This book is almost completely empty. I see only one story."

Returning with a small, wooden box in his hands, his grandfather explained, "That's because the other stories haven't been unlocked yet. First, we need to save the piece of art in this story here. Once we succeed, another story will be revealed. Go on. Read it so we see what it is about."

Wen went back to the first page, and began to read.

In the 16th century, the Italian painter and sculptor, Leonardo da Vinci, created one of the most famous paintings of all times: the Mona Lisa.

This portrait, also known as *La Gioconda*, was left unfinished and unsigned. The identity of the woman in this painting continues to be a mystery. The painting was on display in the Louvre, one of the worlds largest museums, located in Paris, France, when it was stolen in 1911. The thief was never found, and the Mona Lisa vanished forever.

3

"I've heard of this painting, Gramps," Wen said, after he finished reading. "And we've learned about its theft in school. It was so famous because of its mysterious smile."

"Yes," answered Gramps. "And nobody ever knew who this woman in this portrait really was. But come on now. It is our responsibility to save this painting."

"How are we going to do that, Gramps?" Wen asked. "You don't really think I believe that we can travel through time, do you?"

5
The Amser Legacy

"Well," his grandfather responded. "See for yourself." He opened the wooden box and retrieved an ancient-looking amulet. It was the size of an old-fashioned pocket watch. And it was broken. "This amulet holds our family crest and is the key to all times. It can take one of us anywhere in time and place." Wen looked around the library. All the leather-bound books had the image of this family crest on the cover. Wen had never noticed. Until now.

"Gramps, what do all these symbols mean? And why is it broken?"

Carefully tracing the raised contours of the crest with his fingers, Gramps answered, "This here is the Owl

of Athena, the Greek goddess of wisdom and the arts. It wraps its wings protectively around an hourglass, which represents the present as being between the past and the future. We, today, can influence what will be tomorrow by going back in time."

Holding up the amulet, Gramps continued, "Behind the Owl of Athena is a compass that helps us find our way, where and whenever we are."

Gramps pointed at the broken edge of the amulet. "A piece of the amulet is missing. It broke off a long time ago. A man named Vex Hunt has it," Gramps said. "He wants all the art pieces for himself. He follows us wherever we go. But he can only travel through time if one of us, an Amser, is going into the past. If you feel like you're being watched, you probably are. That's when you need to be especially careful. I've never seen his face. But I know he is quite ruthless. You need to watch out for him, Wen!"

Gramps sternly looked at Wen. Placing the string with the amulet around Wen's neck, he said, "Now, listen! This is important. Take good care of this amulet. It is your only way back home." He picked up a little notebook that also had their family crest on its cover. A little pencil was attached to it. "Use this to communicate with me. This is the only way I can help you when you are in the past."

"Wait, Gramps!" Wen interrupted. "You are coming with me, right?"

"I can't, Wen," his grandfather responded. "Each piece of the amulet can transport only one person through time. But don't worry. You won't be alone."

As if she could understand what Gramps just said, Minty came and jumped onto Wen's lap. Gramps patted her gently. "This little girl will come with you. Minty has been doing this for centuries, Wen. Let her guide you." With that, his grandfather took Wen's hand, put it on top of the amulet, squeezed it gently, and said:

"Ars longa, vita brevis.
By my right as an Amser, so I exhort.
Take them to Paris, year 1911,
For art is eternal, and life is short."

Wen felt a slight pressure in his ears. His head started to spin. Faster and faster. Until, suddenly, everything came to a complete halt.

6
Paris, 1911

Wen opened his eyes. Confused, he looked around. He held the dog, but they were no longer sitting in Gramps' library. "Where are we?" Minty licked Wen's face as if to answer him. She wagged her tail and bumped Wen with her nose, urging him to get up from the ground. Then, she suddenly took off. "Wait, Minty!" Wen called after her. He had to hurry if he wanted to keep up.

He followed the dog, past a large poster stuck to the wall of a house. On it, the words "Salon D'Automne – Annual Art Exhibition – Paris 1911" were printed. "Paris? 1911?" Wen said out loud. Didn't Gramps say something about Paris and the year 1911 when he spoke his spell? Could this be real? Did he really travel through time all the way to France?

Wen rubbed his fingers over the amulet that was hanging around his neck. Good! It was still there. He tucked it under his shirt to keep it safe.

It was warm. It must have been very early because only a few horse-drawn carriages clip-clopped their way through the cobble-stoned streets. Their horseshoes echoed loudly through the air. A few old-fashioned automobiles were parked along the side of the roads.

Wen followed Minty down an empty street. She seemed to be following someone. A suspicious-looking man was in the street ahead of them, nervously holding

SALON
D'AUTOMNE
GRAND PALAIS

ÉCLAIRÉ

onto something wrapped in what seemed to be white cloth. What was he carrying? And why was Minty following him?

Wen looked down at himself. His clothes felt scratchy and heavy. What was he wearing? These were not his clothes! Wen was dressed in a white button-down shirt, shorts that were held up with suspenders, black laced boots and dark mid-calf socks. On his head he wore a tweed cap. A leather belt pack was wrapped around his waist. This couldn't be real. Or could it?

7
The Notebook

A loud dinging sound pulled Wen out of his thoughts. A plain-looking, red tram crept its way along the tracks. As soon as it came to a complete stop, the stranger boarded the first of the two cars. Minty jumped onto the second car, looking expectantly at Wen. "I guess I have no choice," Wen said, climbing onto the tram as well.

Wen looked toward the front, trying to make out the stranger in the car ahead of them. The man wore a gray suite and had a mustache. "Who is that man, Minty? And what are we supposed to do?" The Notebook! Remembering his grandfather's words, Wen started looking for the notebook. He found it in his belt pack. *Use this to communicate with me*, his grandfather had said. "Okay," Wen said to himself, "let's see how this works." He took the pencil and wrote:

Who is that man?

He didn't have to wait long. His mouth dropped open in awe as words slowly appeared on the page. This was insane! It really worked! Wen read:

That man is Vincenzo Peruggia, an Italian carpenter that ended up living in France.

Follow him and see where he takes her.
Don't lose him. If you do, she will be gone
forever.

Wen was confused. What was his grandfather talking about? Using his pencil, he quickly dotted down three words:

Gone? Who? Why?

His grandfather responded by writing:

Peruggia has the Mona Lisa. He stole the painting from the Louvre. Nobody will notice that she is missing until tomorrow. By then, it will be too late! He believes that Napoleon (the first emperor of France) stole the painting from Italy and brought her to Paris. And now, Peruggia is planning to take the portrait out of France and return it to Italy. You __must__ prevent this!

Oh man! Wen thought. He was too late. He had not been able to stop the robbery.

As the tram bumped and jostled along on its track, Wen had to hold on to the handrail. It was a bumpy ride. The tram curved its way along the La Seine River,

stopping every so often to let passengers on and off.

Wen scanned the faces of passengers on the tram. "I don't see him anymore, Minty!" Wen suddenly panicked. He got up and stumbled toward the front of the car. Did Peruggia get off the tram without him noticing? Did he lose him?

The tram came to a halt. Wen stuck his head out of the window, trying to find Peruggia. There he was, the man with the mustache and the gray suite. "I see him," Wen said relieved.

"He's getting off," Wen whispered. Looking at Minty, he said, "Let's go, girl!" They hurried off the tram and followed the man without getting too close. The stranger crossed a small canal and finally turned onto a street named Rue de l'Hôpital Saint-Louis. Still holding on to the cloth-covered item, he opened a wooden door that led into a large, gray-looking building. He walked inside.

8

Rescue Mission

"That must be where he lives," Wen said out loud. "Oh, Minty, what should we do?" As if to answer him, Minty wagged her tail and began walking behind the house the thief had disappeared into a few moments earlier. Wen followed. Attached to the back of the house was a rusty fire escape. Minty sat down beside the bottom of the ladder and looked at Wen.

"You want me to climb up there?"

Minty let out a quiet yip.

"Okay. If you think so. Let's see if I can find out what apartment Peruggia lives in."

Wen carefully began climbing up the ladder. "Wait here, Minty. I'll be right..." Wen turned toward the dog, but she was gone. *Where did she go? Never mind!* Wen had to hurry before Peruggia could take the painting someplace else.

Quietly creeping along the wall, he made his way up, carefully peeking through every window he passed. On the second flight up, Wen exclaimed, "There he is!" Wen ducked below the window. Vincenzo Peruggia was in a sparsely-furnished, one-room apartment. As Wen slowly peeked back over the windowsill, he saw Peruggia open up a large chest, take the flat wooden panel on which the Mona Lisa was painted, and put it in the box.

"What a clever guy," Wen said to himself. "He's

hiding the painting under a false bottom in his trunk."

He had to get in somehow. The building seemed old. Maybe he could just try to open the window from the outside. But he would have to wait until Peruggia left his apartment. That could take forever. How long can someone travel through time for, anyway? Was there a time limit? Wen realized that Gramps hadn't explained any of this to him. Wen took a deep breath. *One step at a time,* he thought.

Suddenly, Peruggia jumped out of the chair he was sitting in. "Sacré bleu," he said. "What is this?" Peruggia walked toward his door and pressed his ear against it. Wen could make out loud scratching noises.

What was going on? Peruggia unlocked his door and opened it. *Minty!* Out of the blue, she dashed into the apartment, jumped toward Peruggia and bit into his leg.

"Aaugh!" Peruggia yelped in pain. "Get off of me!" Now having his full attention, Minty released him, turned around and took off down the hallway. Peruggia ran out of his apartment to chase after her.

"This is my chance," Wen realized. His heart was pounding. A million thoughts went through his head. It was now or never. He pulled on the old wooden window frame. It wouldn't budge. Wen pulled harder. Paint began to peel off under his fingers, but then, with a screeching sound, the window panes swung open. Success!

Wen quickly climbed into the room. He had to hurry. Peruggia could come back any second. Wen made his way over to the bed and pulled the wooden trunk out from under it. He opened the lid and lifted up the false bottom. There she was: the Mona Lisa, still wrapped in the white cloth. Hastily, Wen lifted the priceless painting out of the trunk, replaced the false bottom, and closed the top.

Suddenly, he heard heavy footsteps approaching from the hallway. Peruggia was coming back! Quickly, Wen pushed the trunk back under the bed, grabbed the painting, and climbed back out of the window. He barely had time to close the window back up and dodge out of sight before Peruggia dashed into his apartment. Peruggia was furious. Minty must have escaped.

9
First Encounter

Quickly, Wen climbed back down the fire escape. He was still shaking. With trembling hands, he held onto the Mona Lisa. He got her! As he reached the street again, he saw some movement out of the corner of his eye. But it was too late. As soon as Wen turned his head, a man jumped out of the nearby bushes and grabbed the cloth-covered painting, trying to wrench it out of Wen's hand. But Wen held on tightly.

"No," he shouted. "Let go!" He tore the painting free from the stranger's grip and took off running as fast as he could. Wen's feet had never moved quicker. He could hear the man's heavy breathing and his shoes hitting the pavement. But Wen didn't dare to look back. He turned sharply into a small alley. He saw a large dumpster. Wen dove between the dumpster and some large cardboard boxes stacked next to it. Trying to muffle his heavy breathing, he hoped the stranger hadn't seen him run this way. He heard the footsteps coming closer. They slowed down and came to a complete halt near the dumpster. Had the stranger seen him? Wen held his breath. Slowly, the footsteps moved away from his hiding place and soon, were completely gone.

Wen blew out a sigh of relief. He was safe. But all of a sudden, the cardboard boxes began to move. Wen

almost shrieked out loud until he realized it was Minty. She stuck her nose into his face and gave him a good lick. "Minty, you found me!" Wen said. "Did you just see this? I think I just had my first encounter with Vex Hunt. It's time for us to get out of here!"

10
Bringing Her Home

"You are unbelievable, Minty!" Wen said, while they started walking. He patted the dog. "I cannot believe we got the Mona Lisa out of Peruggia's apartment!" They quickly walked back the way they'd come earlier. "Let's let Gramps know we have the painting. He'll tell us what to do next." Wen took out the notebook from his belt pack and wrote:

We've got her. What now? Police?

Wen thought he should let the police know about Peruggia. After all, he was a thief and just tried to steal Leonardo da Vinci's masterpiece. His grandfather responded promptly:

Well done, Wen! But NO police!!! When traveling through time, we must try to have as little contact with people of that time as possible. The less contact, the less interference. Remember that, Wen! It's very important.

Return to the museum. Bring her in the same way Peruggia took her out. Use the side entrance to the east. This place is not well guarded, especially on Mondays when the museum is closed to the public. Take advantage of that.

Wen put the notebook back into his pack. Wen and Minty made their way back to the tram that took them all the way to the Louvre. The streets were a lot busier than before. Horse shoes were tapping and automobile engines were running. People were out and about, getting ready to begin their hectic day in a big city.

Wen and Minty got off the tram in front of the Louvre and walked toward the side of the massive museum building, looking for the door Peruggia had presumably used earlier. He found one that was unlocked and unguarded. This had to be the one. No security safeguarding any of the art pieces within the grand halls. Wen made his way through the large museum halls, following the signs to the gallery the Mona Lisa was usually displayed in. Minty followed closely behind. There it was, the empty spot with an empty hook the painting was meant to hang on.

"This should have never happened," Wen said aloud, "we have to do something to prevent this from happening again!" Taking the notebook and pen out of his pack, he wrote something on one of the pages. He tore the page out of the book. Then, he placed the still-wrapped painting onto the floor below its hook and attached the note to it.

"Time for us to go back home," Wen said, turning to Minty. "But how?" Just as he was about to write down his question, the verse that would bring them home appeared in the notebook. Wen smiled. *I can always count on Gramps*, he thought. Taking the amulet out from under his shirt, Wen put his arm around Minty and said:

> **"Ars longa, vita brevis.**
> **By my right as an Amser, so I exhort.**
> **Take us back home where we belong,**
> **For art is eternal, and life is short."**

Wen felt slight pressure in his ears. His head started to spin. Faster and faster. Until suddenly, once again, everything came to a complete halt.

11
Back Home

Wen opened his eyes. He and Minty were back in Gramps' library! He wore his own clothes again. Hugging Minty vigorously, Wen turned to his grandfather who was still sitting in the same spot he had been earlier, what seemed like hours ago.

"I'm back!" Wen grinned. "Was this for real, Gramps, or was I dreaming?"

"As real as I'm sitting here," his grandfather answered with a gentle smile on his face. "You did well, Wen! You went on your very first time travel today."

Lifting the book they had read earlier from the nearby coffee table, his grandfather handed it to Wen. Wen opened it up to the page he had looked at before Gramps had spoken the time spell earlier that day. When he looked down at the pages, the last part of the previous writing vanished right in front of his eyes.

"Gramps, look!" he exclaimed. "The writing is disappearing."

"Watch closely," his grandfather said. "Things have been changed because of you, Wen. Let's see what the writing says now." Leaning over the book, both read the slowly appearing words.

In the 16th century, the Italian painter and sculptor, Leonardo da Vinci, created

one of the most famous paintings of all times: the Mona Lisa. This portrait, also known as *La Gioconda*, was left unfinished and unsigned. The identity of the woman in this painting continues to be a mystery. The painting is on display in the Louvre, one of the world's largest museums, located in Paris, France. Security measures were dramatically increased in 1911, after a Parisian artist named Louis Béroud found a note attached to the displaced painting.

> If it was this easy for us to take her off the hook, it wouldn't be very hard to take her altogether. Take care of the Mona Lisa. She is one of the worlds most prized possessions.

No one knows who left this note, but security has been increased to safeguard all paintings throughout the museum.

"I guess we just added to the painting's mysteries," Gramps said.

"What do you mean?" asked Wen.

"Well, there are all these uncertainties about the Mona Lisa. It's unsigned. Undated. No confirmed identity. And now they found this mysterious note." Gramps smiled. "All everyone is left with are these lips that smile and these eyes that shine."

"The painting does look beautiful, Gramps! I'm glad we were able to save it. Let's see if we unlocked the next story," Wen said as he turned the page. Little by little, he saw new text and images appear. Wen read aloud:

In 1889, Dutch painter Vincent van Gogh painted one of his finest works: the Starry Night. The painting shows the view from his bedroom window in France, just before sunrise.

After its completion, van Gogh sent it off to his brother Theo, an art dealer in Paris. During its transfer, the train carrying the painting was robbed. Along with all the cargo in the mail car of the train, the painting was stolen and never recovered.

4

5

"Looks like we're going back to France," Wen said, turning to Minty. "I hope you don't get train-sick…"

AFTERWORD:
MONA LISA'S THEFT IN 1911: AN
UNBELIEVABLE TRUE STORY

Though Wen and his family are made up, the major events of the story are true. Leonardo da Vinci's Mona Lisa really was stolen from the Louvre in 1911 by an Italian named Vincenzo Peruggia. After keeping the painting hidden in a trunk in his apartment for two years, Peruggia returned to Italy with it to sell it to an art gallery in Florence. The owner of the gallery contacted the police, and Peruggia was arrested.

It isn't entirely clear why he decided to steal this particular painting. What we do know is that the disappearance of the Mona Lisa made this painting even more famous than it was before. More than 6 million people visit her in Paris every year. She has become the most famous painting of all time.

ABOUT THE AUTHOR

Yvonne Jones was born in former East Germany to a German mother and a Vietnamese father. Thus, she spent an inordinate amount of her youth nosing through books that she shouldn't have been reading, and watching movies that she shouldn't have been watching. It was a good childhood.

She currently lives in Texas with her husband and their two sons. In theory, she is working on her next children's book. In reality, she is probably being tickled or busy pretend-playing with her little ones. She can be found online at **www.Yvonne-Jones.com**.

CPSIA information can be obtained
at www.ICGtesting.com
Printed in the USA
LVHW092351050821
694688LV00004B/208

9 780997 025408